Whose Hat Is That?

by RON ROY

photographs by
ROSMARIE HAUSHERR

Clarion Books
New York

For Mary Gambill, a good friend to animals, children, and writers.

R.R.

Photographer's Note:

My thanks to all the parents, children, teachers, and friends who have participated in photo-sessions, helped with valuable information, or lent me their hats and props for this book. Special thanks to: New England Culinary Institute, Montpelier, Vermont; Metro Bicycle Stores, New York City; George Gilbert, magician, New York City; Amtrak; Barnet & Peacham Volunteer Fire Department, Vermont; Dutch Girl Painters, New York City; New York Racing Association, Inc.; Allan Greenleaf, Peacham, Vermont; Lyndon Institute football team, Vermont; New York City Park & Recreation Department; New York City Department of Transportation, Bureau of Highways; the Marunas family; Dr. Kim Kahng; Cody McCone; the Fraiman family; the Hildreth family; Corlears School, New York City; Nazareth Nursery School, New York City.

Clarion Books
a Houghton Mifflin Company imprint
215 Park Avenue South, New York, NY 10003
Text copyright © 1987 by Ron Roy
Photographs copyright © 1987 by Rosmarie Hausherr

Library of Congress Cataloging-in-Publication Data
Roy, Ron, 1940-
    Whose hat is that?
      Summary: Text and photographs portray the appearance
and function of eighteen types of hats, including a
top hat, jockey's cap, and football helmet.
      1. Hats — Juvenile literature.   [1. Hats]   I. Hausherr,
Rosmarie, ill.   II. Title.
GT2110.R69   1987   391'.43   86-17553
ISBN 0-89919-446-X   PA ISBN 0-395-54429-7

HOR   10 9 8 7

Do you have a favorite hat? Why do you wear it? Many people wear hats to protect their heads. Others wear hats to pretend they are someone else. Some people wear hats just for fun!

You will see many different hats in this book. Maybe you will even see your own favorite hat! Before you begin to read, why not put on your special hat?

Who wears a straw hat
with a wide brim?

ple who sit or play in the hot sun often wear a hat woven
w. The wide brim of the hat shades the face and protects it fr
ourn. Straw hats are lightweight and cool. Do you wear a str
in the summertime?

Why does this hat
cover the face?

ple who play or work outside in cold weather must dress warmly.
.s wool hat keeps the head, nose, ears, chin, and cheeks warm.
. can breathe right through the wool. Wearing this hat, you can
l your friends. They won't know who you are!

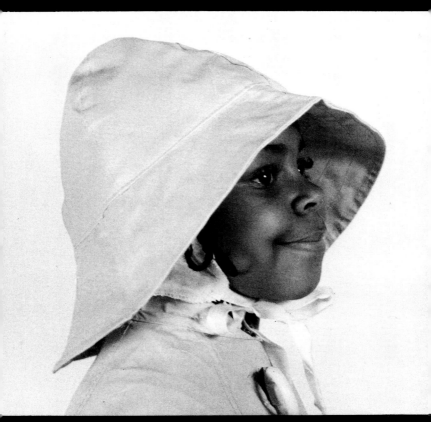

Who wears a waterproof hat that dips down in the back?

ny people wear these hats when it rains. Workers who build
air streets and highways often wear these waterproof hats,
e hats are bright yellow, so people driving in traffic will see
kers. Rainwater drips off the sloping rim in the back instea
ing down the person's neck. On windy days, these hats car
l under the chin. Who wants to chase a hat on a windy, rainy c

Why does this hat have a net
that covers the face and neck?

is is a beekeeper's hat. When beekeepers collect honey from t.
hives, they may get stung. To protect themselves from
gs, beekeepers hang nets made of fine mesh from their spe
s. The bees cannot fly through the tiny holes in the mesh. A t
ng at the bottom stops the bees from flying under the net.

Who wears a hat shaped
like a turtle's shell?

Builders must wear these hard hats when they work on construction sites. Builders work with heavy materials. They move lumber and steel, pour concrete, and lay bricks. The hard hat will protect the worker if something heavy falls on him or her. Hard hats also protect the workers if they accidentally bump their heads.

Why is this hat covered
with colored splotches?

...ve you ever gotten paint in your hair? If you have, you know ...nters wear these hats. Painting is messy work! These caps c... ...hair and shield the face from paint splatters. Sometimes pair... ...given these hats for free when they buy paint. They throw... ...s away when the paint job is finished.

Who wears this tall, white hat?

ly the chef, who is in charge of the kitchen, wears the tall, wh
The cooks wear floppy hats. Together, they prepare food i
aurant. The heat from the stoves makes the kitchen hot. If
f and cooks perspire, the hatbands keep the sweat from dripp
their eyes. The hats also stop hair from falling into the food

Who wears a stretchy rubber cap
to cover the hair?

ny people wear thin rubber caps when they swim. The caps ┊
┊ the hair from salt in the ocean and chlorine in swimming pc┊
┊ hats also keep the swimmers' hair out of their eyes. Swimn┊
┊ race can swim faster with their hair covered. They slip thro┊
┊ water like seals!

Who wears a snug helmet
that buckles under the chin?

Jockeys wear these helmets for protection when they ride in horse races. If a jockey is thrown from a horse, the hard helmet will protect his or her head. The straps and buckle keep the helmet in place. Look closely and you will see that the helmet is covered with a silk cap. This is so the helmet will match the jockey's colorful riding outfit.

Who wears a paper cap that
completely covers the hair?

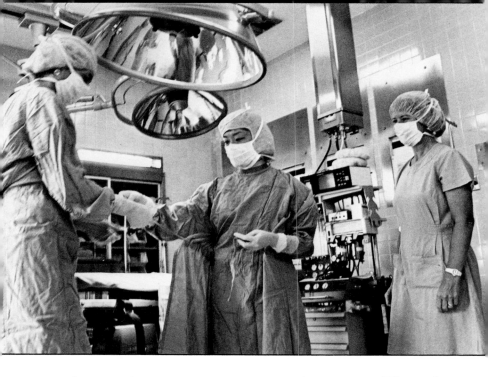

geons and operating-room nurses wear these caps. They also
r face masks, gowns, and rubber gloves. People who work in op-
ting rooms wear this clothing so that germs from their hair,
at, or breath do not get on the patients. The caps, as well as the
sks and gloves, are thrown away after the operation. The gowns
washed and sterilized to make them free from germs. Then the
ns can be used again.

Who wears a helmet
with sloping edges?

nting a fire can be very dangerous work. Firefighters wear h
mets to protect their heads and necks from sparks, falling
s, and water. They also wear fire-resistant suits. Some f
ters lower face shields on their helmets to keep sparks out
r eyes. One firefighter in the picture wears a special mask. I
nected to an oxygen tank worn on his back. If he goes int
ning building, he can still breathe, even in the heavy sm
sed by the fire.

Who would wear this elegant, tall hat?

ng ago, men wore these hats on special occasions, such as fa
ties, weddings, or important meetings. They are called top h
w many people wear these elegant hats. For example, so
cers wear top hats when they perform. Magicians sometimes
hats when they do tricks. What a good place to hide flow
ds, or scarves!

Which is the most popular cap
of all?

s the baseball player's cap. Players wear these caps to keep
r out of their eyes. The stiff visor on the front of the cap sh
eyes from the sun. The caps are soft so players can stuff t
o a pocket. Most baseball caps have the team's name or initial
front. Do you wear a baseball cap?

Why does this helmet have bars
in front of the face?

s is a football helmet. Football is an exciting sport, but it can
dangerous. Players get knocked to the ground and often k
r heads. These strong helmets prevent injury to the play
d and neck. The bars in the face guard protect the nose, mo
jaw. The helmets are padded on the inside and fastened secu
n the chin guard. Can you guess why these helmets have h
the ears?

Why does this cap have a special badge over the visor?

s cap is part of a uniform. The badge says Conductor. W
n travelers need a conductor's help, they look for a mar
nan wearing this special cap. Uniform caps are also worn
ts, police officers, bus drivers, mail deliverers, or others wh
is helping people. The uniform cap is like a sign that asks, "M
> you?"

Who wears a western hat
with a wide, curved brim?

25

n and women who work around horses and cattle on ranc
r these hats. Ranches and rodeos are dusty places. The w
ns keep dust off the workers' heads and sun out of their eyes. '
ved brims catch rainwater so it doesn't run down their back
atband inside the hat absorbs perspiration before it drips
r eyes. How many western hats can you see in this picture?

When do you wear a hat
decorated with flowers and lace?

may want to wear a special hat when you celebrate a spe···
···t. Some people wear dressy hats to parties. Many people w···
···n to church or synagogue. Others like to dress up to celebr···
···coming of spring! Some people decorate their own hats. T···
···ribbons, lace, flowers, or even berries. How would you decor···
···ecial hat?

Who wears a flat cap with a tassel hanging on the side?

hen students graduate from school, they often wear these
h gowns at their graduation ceremony. Before the ceremony
's tassel hangs on the right side of the student's face. At the s
ment near the end of the ceremony, each student moves the
to the left side. This means the students have graduated. T
s their caps into the air. Hurray!

DATE DUE

GAYLORD   PRINTED IN U.S.A